cloverleaf books™

Stories with Character

# In It Together
## A Story of Fairness

**Kristin Johnson**

illustrated by **Mike Byrne**

MILLBROOK PRESS • MINNEAPOLIS

To my friend and fellow writer
Sarah Rose —K.J.


To Oscar & Harry —M.B.

Millbrook Press
A division of Lerner Publishing Group, Inc.
241 First Avenue North
Minneapolis, MN 55401 USA

For reading levels and more information, look up this title at
www.lernerbooks.com.

**Library of Congress Cataloging-in-Publication Data**

The Cataloging-in-Publication Data for *In It Together: A Story of
Fairness* is on file at the Library of Congress.
ISBN 978-1-5124-8649-0 (lib. bdg.)
ISBN 978-1-5415-1068-5 (pbk.)
ISBN 978-1-5124-9823-3 (EB pdf)

LC record available at https://lccn.loc.gov/2017014394

Manufactured in the United States of America
2-46345-33213-7/2/2018

# TABLE OF CONTENTS

# Chapter One
# I'm in Charge

Today at school, we're learning about animals.

Our teacher, Mrs. Rose, splits us into groups. We're going to do research in the library. Each group will choose an animal and make a poster about it.

Mrs. Rose made me our group's leader!

"Let's research a cheetah," I tell my group.

"Let's do a bat instead!" Layla says.
Noah and Grace agree.

I'm the leader, so I tell my group that I should get to choose.

"You have to listen to us too, Justin," Grace
says as we line up to go to the library.

"Yeah! This isn't fair!" adds Noah.

# Chapter Two

# Compromising

"All right," I say when we get to the library.
"We can do a bat, but is it OK if I draw it?"
Everyone agrees.

Layla wants to look for books about bats.

"I should do it," Noah says. "I'm a fast reader."
"But it was my idea," says Layla.

"Why don't you
look for books
together?" I say.

They're both happy with that!

Compromising is a part of being fair.

13

# Chapter Three

# Out of Control

Back at our table, Grace is reading a joke book.

"Why aren't you working on our project?" I ask.

"No one gave me anything to do," she says.

I ask Grace to help me gather art supplies.

MAKERSPACE

Fairness means
including everyone.

15

We set out the supplies, and Noah and Layla return with books.

They start arguing about who gets to write with the red marker first.

"We don't have markers for everyone," Grace says. "You have to share!"

"Guys, we're never going to finish this if we don't **treat each other fairly**," I say.

Noah lets go of the marker. "You're right."

# Chapter Four

# Getting It Together

"How about I do the writing, and you both can tell me what you want to say?" Grace offers.

Noah and Layla share what they learned with Grace. I start drawing the bat.

Finally, everyone is in it together!

"Time's up!" Mrs. Rose says.

Our project isn't done yet. I tell Mrs. Rose that we didn't finish our poster.

Then Grace adds, "But that's because we weren't being fair at first."

"By the end, we all worked together," says Layla.

Noah adds, "We didn't finish, but everyone got to participate."

"It's fantastic that you learned to work together," Mrs. Rose tells us. She lets us present our poster. She even tells the class that my group and I make great role models for fairness!

# Fairness Chart

You can make sure there's fairness in your home or classroom!
Think of a part of your life where being fair can sometimes be tricky.
Create a chart that helps you make sure everyone has a turn.

## What You Will Need
a ruler
markers
a sheet of paper
other art supplies, such as glitter glue or
  colored paper scraps
clothespins

**Fairness Chart**
Make beds
Feed dog
Clean room
Wash dishes
Take trash out
Sort laundry
Pick pizza toppings

## What You Will Do

1)  Using your ruler, draw lines from one end of
    the paper to the other. Leave space between
    each line so you have room to write. You can
    label the top of your paper with a title, such
    as "Fairness Chart."

2)  In each of the spaces, write down the chores,
    toys, or whatever you'd like to be split up
    fairly. You can use markers and other supplies to color and decorate the
    spaces.

3)  Write your name on the flat side of a clothespin. On the other
    clothespins, write down the names of your siblings, your classmates, or
    your entire family.

4)  Clip the clothespins to the side of the paper. Put each person's name in
    a different space. Your fairness chart is ready to go! You can move the
    names around throughout the day or once a week.

# GLOSSARY

**compromising:** when people in a disagreement each give up some of what they want

**including:** allowing everyone to be a part of something

**participate:** be involved in

**research:** collecting information about a subject

**role model:** a person whose behavior is imitated by others

## BOOKS

**Donovan, Sandy. *When Is It My Turn? A Book about Fairness.* Minneapolis: Lerner Publications, 2014.** Read about real-life examples of fairness in class, on the playground, and in other situations. How would you make things fair?

**Skinner, Daphne. *Albert Keeps Score.* New York: Kane, 2012.** Check out this story about Albert, who wants to make sure his sister never gets anything more than he does but learns that sometimes 0 is better than 1!

## WEBSITES

**How to Be a Good Sport**
http://kidshealth.org/en/kids/good-sport.html
Take some lessons from the world of sports on how to play fair and be treated fairly. You can also watch a video of former baseball star Cal Ripken Jr. talking about being able to win and lose.

**No Fair**
http://worksheetplace.com/mf_pdf/No-Fair.pdf
Use this worksheet to think about what fairness means to you.